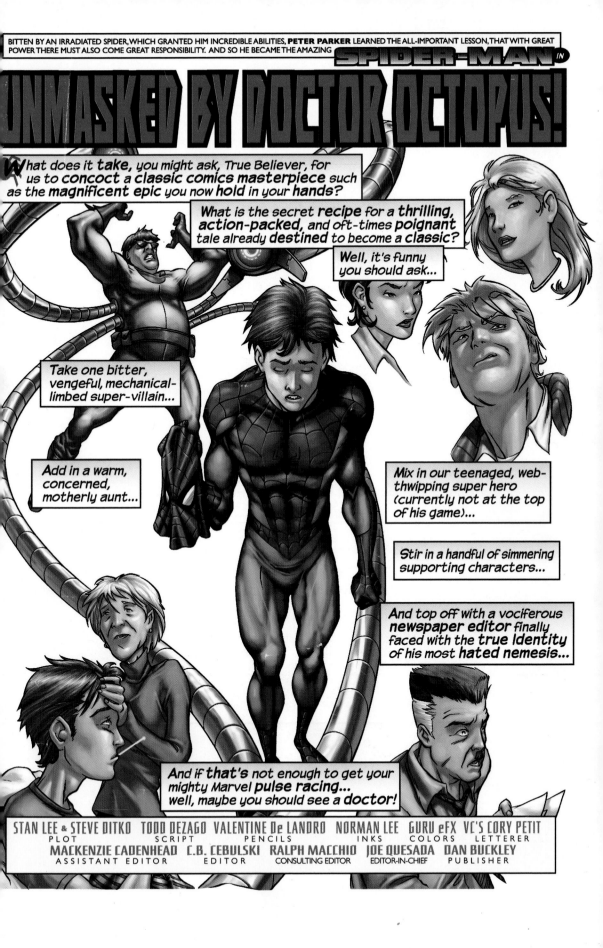

BITTEN BY AN IRRADIATED SPIDER, WHICH GRANTED HIM INCREDIBLE ABILITIES, **PETER PARKER** LEARNED THE ALL-IMPORTANT LESSON, THAT WITH GREAT POWER THERE MUST ALSO COME GREAT RESPONSIBILITY. AND SO HE BECAME THE AMAZING **SPIDER-MAN** _IN_

UNMASKED BY DOCTOR OCTOPUS!

What does it **take**, you might ask, True Believer, for us to **concoct** a **classic comics masterpiece** such as the magnificent epic you now **hold** in your **hands**?

What is the secret **recipe** for a thrilling, **action-packed**, and oft-times **poignant** tale already **destined** to become a **classic**?

Well, it's funny you should ask...

Take one bitter, vengeful, mechanical-limbed super-villain...

Add in a warm, concerned, motherly aunt...

Mix in our teenaged, web-thwipping super hero (currently not at the top of his game)...

Stir in a handful of simmering supporting characters...

And top off with a vociferous **newspaper editor** finally faced with the **true identity** of his most **hated nemesis**...

And if **that's** not enough to get your mighty Marvel **pulse racing**... well, maybe you should see a **doctor**!

STAN LEE & STEVE DITKO	TODD DEZAGO	VALENTINE De LANDRO	NORMAN LEE	GURU eFX	VC'S CORY PETIT
PLOT	SCRIPT	PENCILS	INKS	COLORS	LETTERER

MACKENZIE CADENHEAD	C.B. CEBULSKI	RALPH MACCHIO	JOE QUESADA	DAN BUCKLEY
ASSISTANT EDITOR	EDITOR	CONSULTING EDITOR	EDITOR-IN-CHIEF	PUBLISHER

VISIT US AT

www.abdopub.com

Spotlight, a division of ABDO Publishing Company Inc., is the school and library distributor of the Marvel Entertainment books.

Library bound edition © 2006

Library of Congress Cataloging-in-Publication Data

Unmasked by Doctor Octopus!

ISBN 1-59961-010-8   (Reinforced Library Bound Edition)

All Spotlight books are reinforced library binding and manufactured in the United States of America

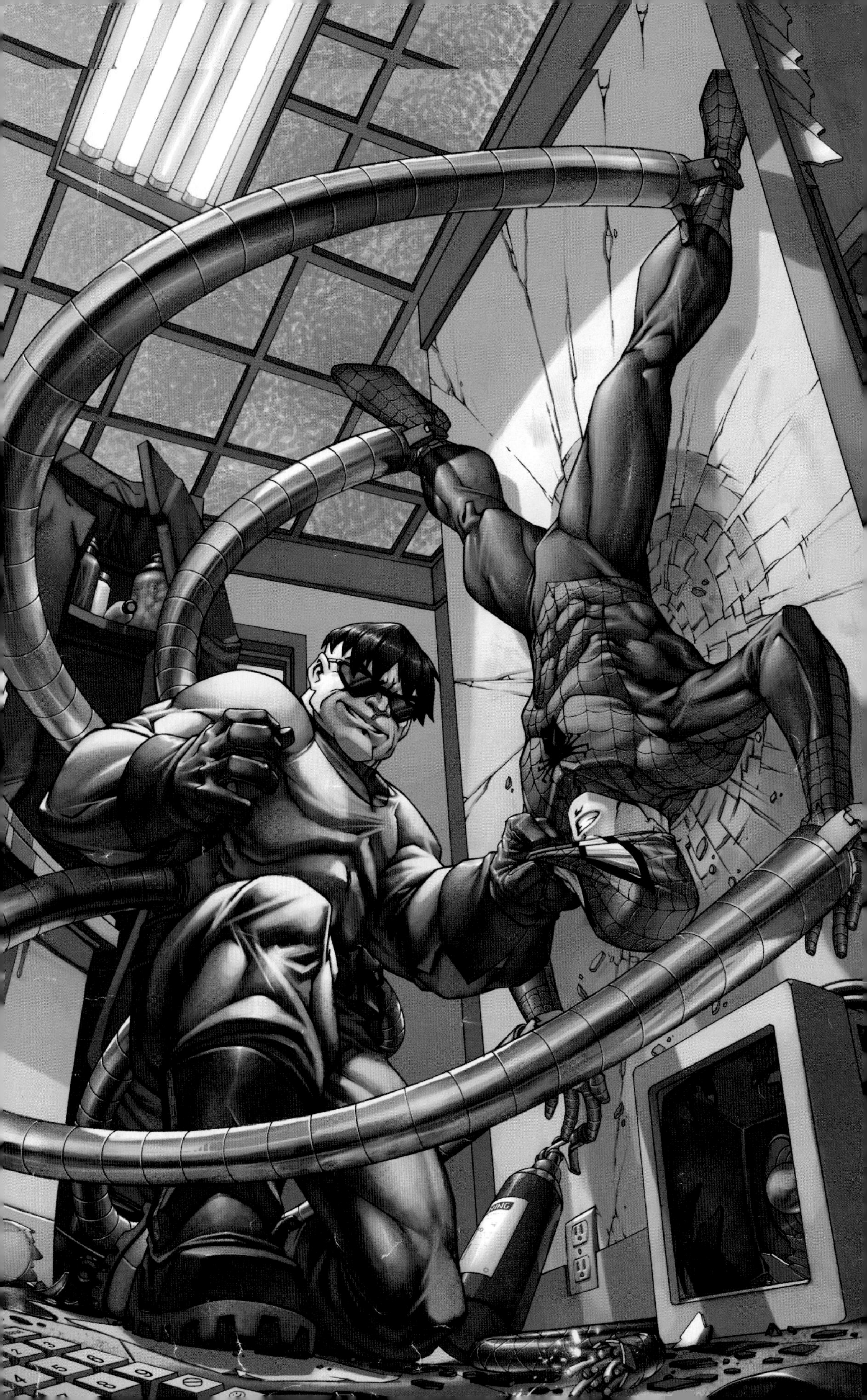

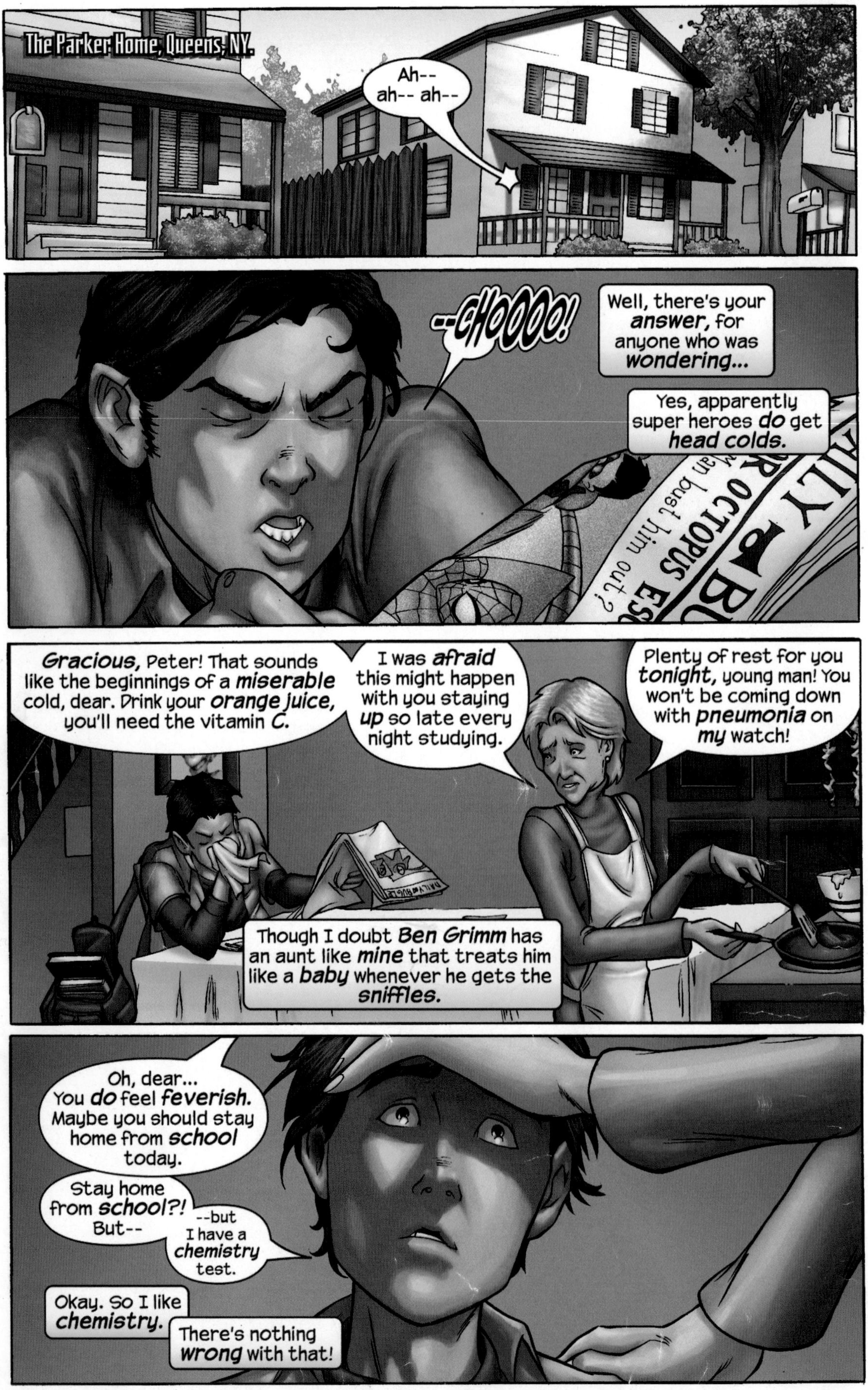
The Parker Home, Queens, NY.
Ah-- ah-- ah--
--CHOOOO!
Well, there's your answer, for anyone who was wondering...
Yes, apparently super heroes do get head colds.
Gracious, Peter! That sounds like the beginnings of a miserable cold, dear. Drink your orange juice, you'll need the vitamin C.
I was afraid this might happen with you staying up so late every night studying.
Plenty of rest for you tonight, young man! You won't be coming down with pneumonia on my watch!
Though I doubt Ben Grimm has an aunt like mine that treats him like a baby whenever he gets the sniffles.
Oh, dear... You do feel feverish. Maybe you should stay home from school today.
Stay home from school?! But--
--but I have a chemistry test.
Okay. So I like chemistry.
There's nothing wrong with that!

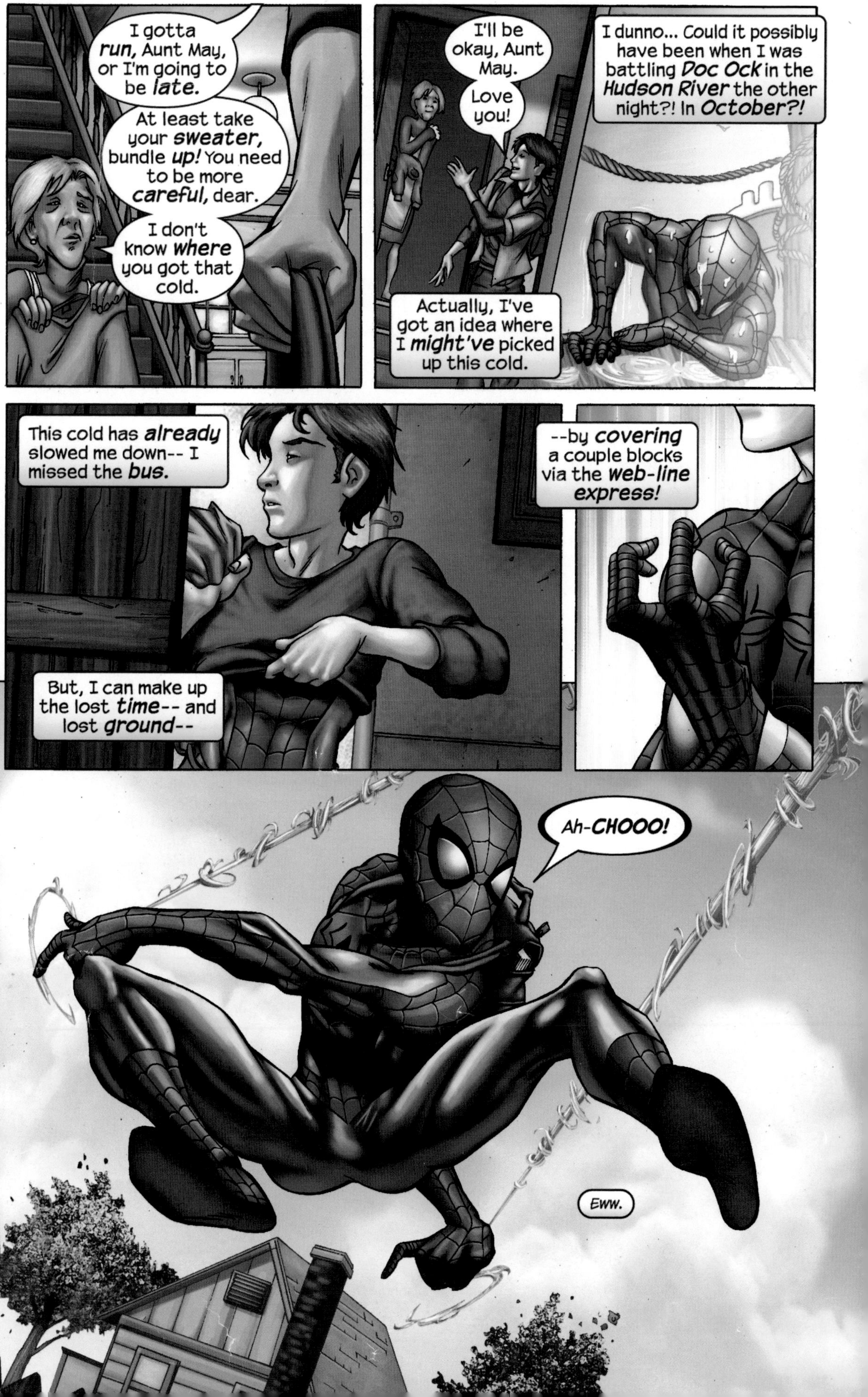
I gotta run, Aunt May, or I'm going to be late.
At least take your sweater, bundle up! You need to be more careful, dear.
I don't know where you got that cold.
I'll be okay, Aunt May.
Love you!
Actually, I've got an idea where I might've picked up this cold.
I dunno... Could it possibly have been when I was battling Doc Ock in the Hudson River the other night?! In October?!
This cold has already slowed me down-- I missed the bus.
But, I can make up the lost time-- and lost ground--
--by covering a couple blocks via the web-line express!
Ah-CHOOO!
Eww.

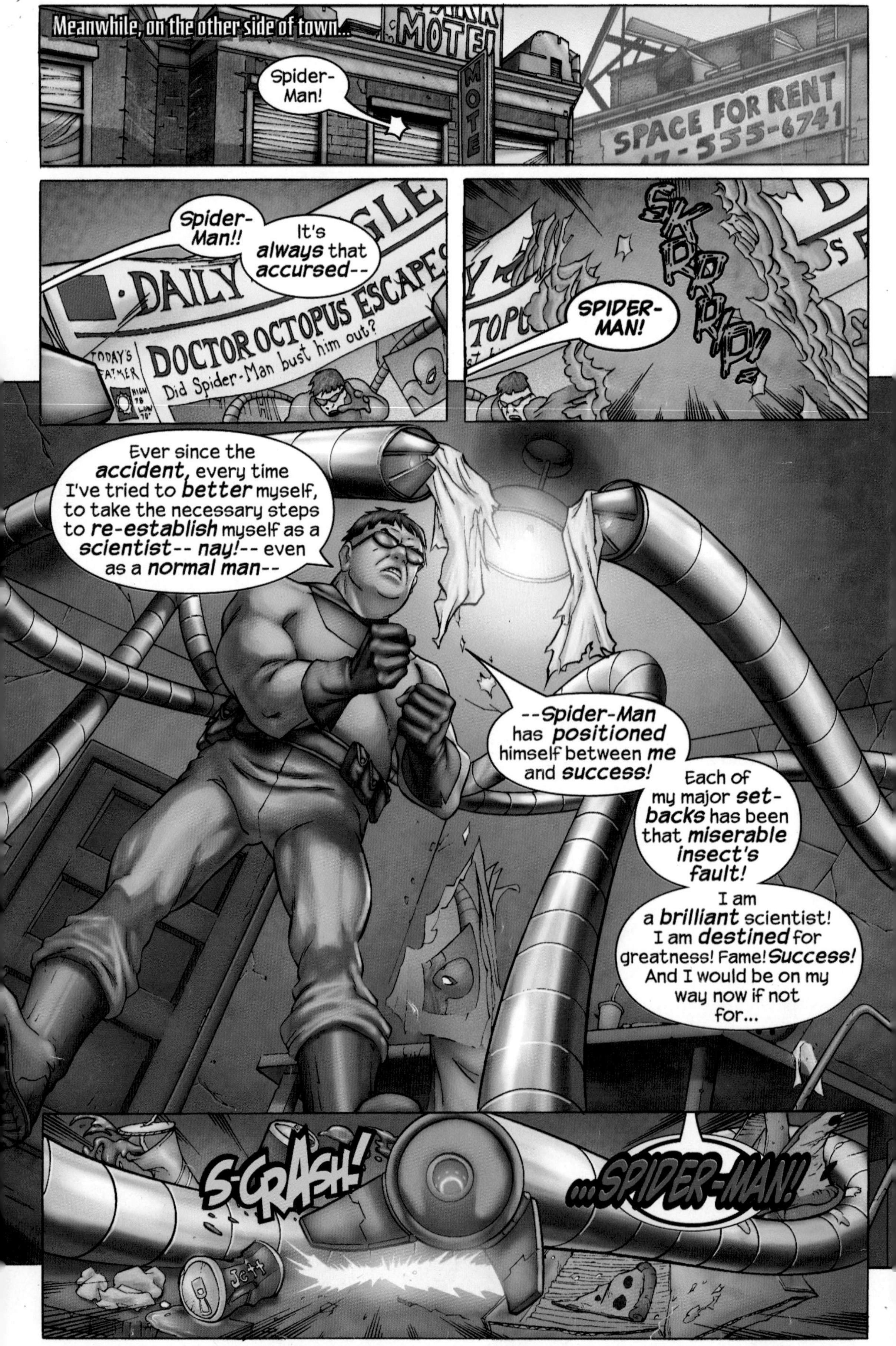

Meanwhile, on the other side of town...
MOTEL
Spider-Man!
SPACE FOR RENT
Spider-Man!!
It's always that accursed--
DAILY BUGLE
DOCTOR OCTOPUS ESCAPES
Did Spider-Man bust him out?
SKRRRIIIP!
SPIDER-MAN!
Ever since the accident, every time I've tried to better myself, to take the necessary steps to re-establish myself as a scientist-- nay!-- even as a normal man--
--Spider-Man has positioned himself between me and success!
Each of my major set-backs has been that miserable insect's fault!
I am a brilliant scientist! I am destined for greatness! Fame! Success! And I would be on my way now if not for...
S-CRASH!
...SPIDER-MAN!

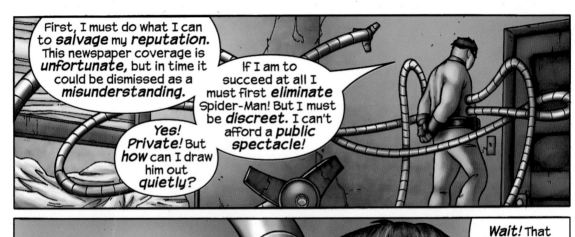

First, I must do what I can to **salvage** my **reputation.** This newspaper coverage is **unfortunate,** but in time it could be dismissed as a **misunderstanding.**

If I am to succeed at all I must first **eliminate** Spider-Man! But I must be **discreet.** I can't afford a **public spectacle!**

Yes! Private! But **how** can I draw him out **quietly?**

Wait! That **girl**... that kid's **sister**... was her name... **Betty?**

He **knew** her... knew her **name**... knew that she worked at...

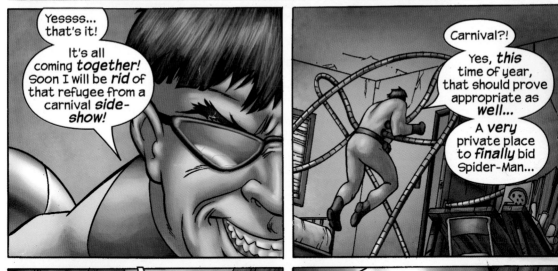

Yessss... that's it! It's all coming **together!** Soon I will be **rid** of that refugee from a carnival **side-show!**

Carnival?! Yes, **this** time of year, that should prove appropriate as **well**...

A **very** private place to **finally** bid Spider-Man...

Farewell!

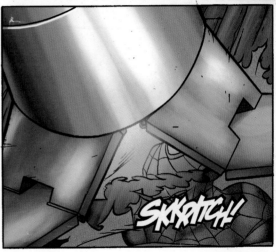

SKKRTCH!

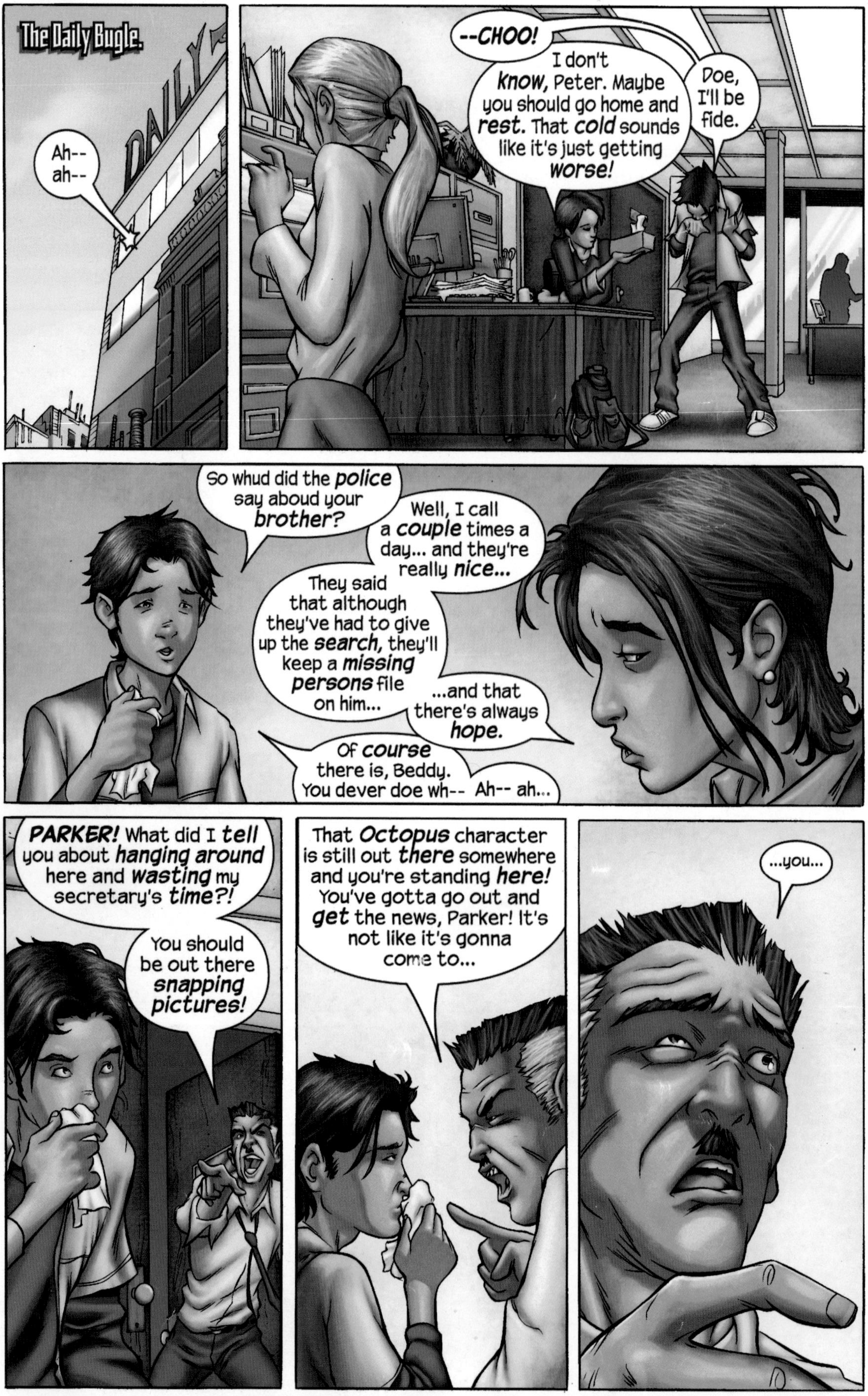
The Daily Bugle.
Ah-- ah--
--CHOO!
I don't know, Peter. Maybe you should go home and rest. That cold sounds like it's just getting worse!
Doe, I'll be fide.
So whud did the police say aboud your brother?
Well, I call a couple times a day... and they're really nice...
They said that although they've had to give up the search, they'll keep a missing persons file on him...
...and that there's always hope.
Of course there is, Beddy. You dever doe wh-- Ah-- ah...
PARKER! What did I tell you about hanging around here and wasting my secretary's time?!
You should be out there snapping pictures!
That Octopus character is still out there somewhere and you're standing here! You've gotta go out and get the news, Parker! It's not like it's gonna come to...
...you...

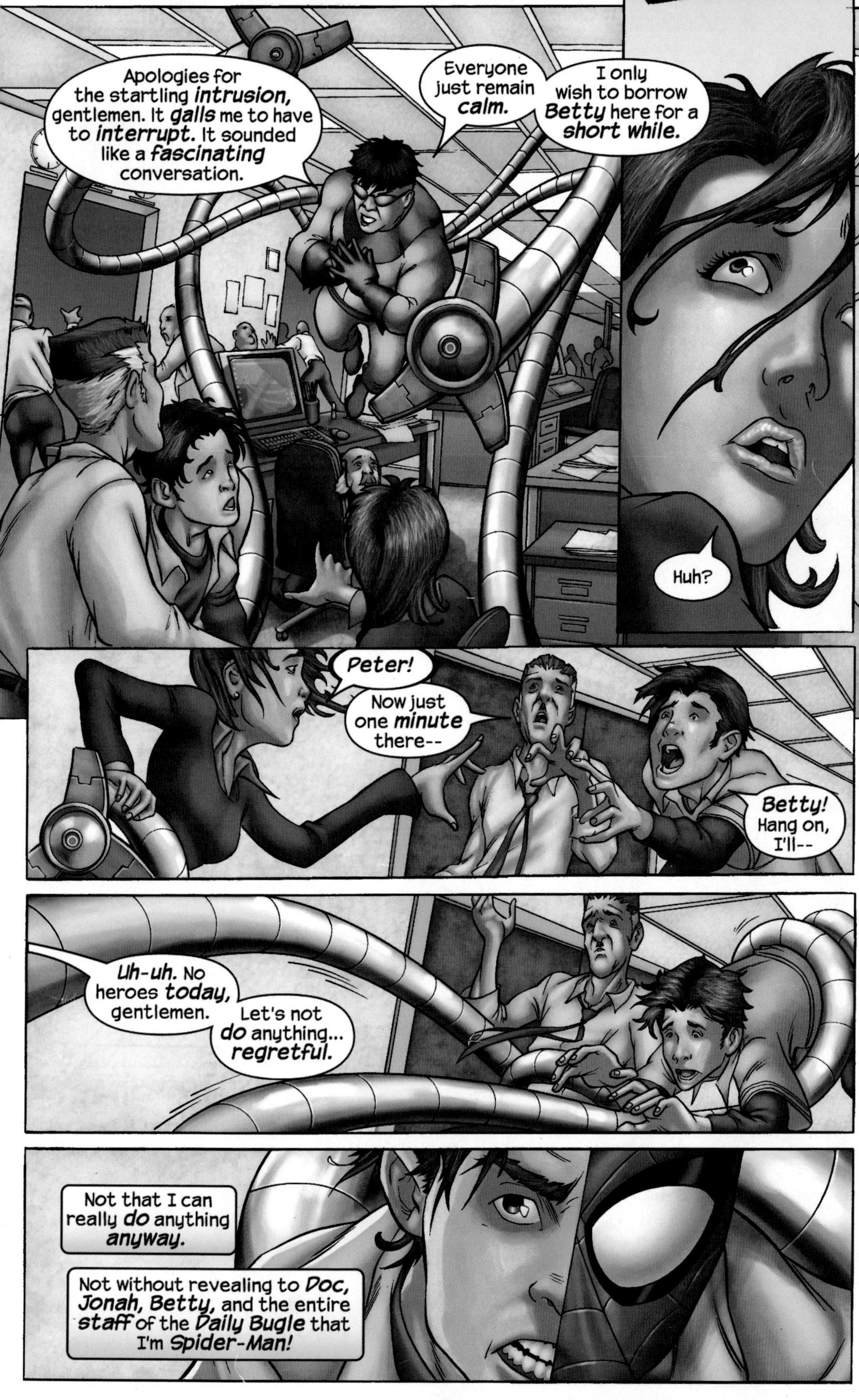
Apologies for the startling *intrusion,* gentlemen. It *galls* me to have to *interrupt.* It sounded like a *fascinating* conversation.
Everyone just remain *calm.*
I only wish to borrow *Betty* here for a *short while.*
Huh?
Peter!
Now just one *minute* there--
Betty! Hang on, I'll--
Uh-uh. No heroes *today,* gentlemen.
Let's not *do* anything... *regretful.*
Not that I can really *do* anything *anyway.*
Not without revealing to *Doc, Jonah, Betty,* and the entire *staff* of the *Daily Bugle* that I'm *Spider-Man!*

You, I *do* wish to speak with, Jameson. Listen. I'll keep it very *simple.*

I want you to contact *Spider-Man.* I want you to use your *paper* to do it. The *late edition.* I want you to tell him to *come* to you. I *don't* want anyone else to *know* about this.

I don't wish to attract any *undue* attention.

When he comes here, you tell him that if he wishes to see Miss *Betty* again, he'll meet me at *Coney Island* at *8:30* tonight. *Alone.* If anyone *else* comes, it's off.

If the *authorities* show up, it's *very* off. Have I made myself *clear?*

Uhn!

THUD!

Actually, Jameson, if you truly *hate* Spider-Man as much as you say in the *paper,* you might even be *tickled* with what I have *planned* for that *menace!*

Late edition?! I've got to... got to...

I've... I've got to go... go get my camera...

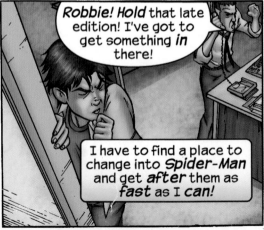

Robbie! *Hold* that late edition! I've got to get something *in* there!

I have to find a place to change into *Spider-Man* and get *after* them as fast as I *can!*

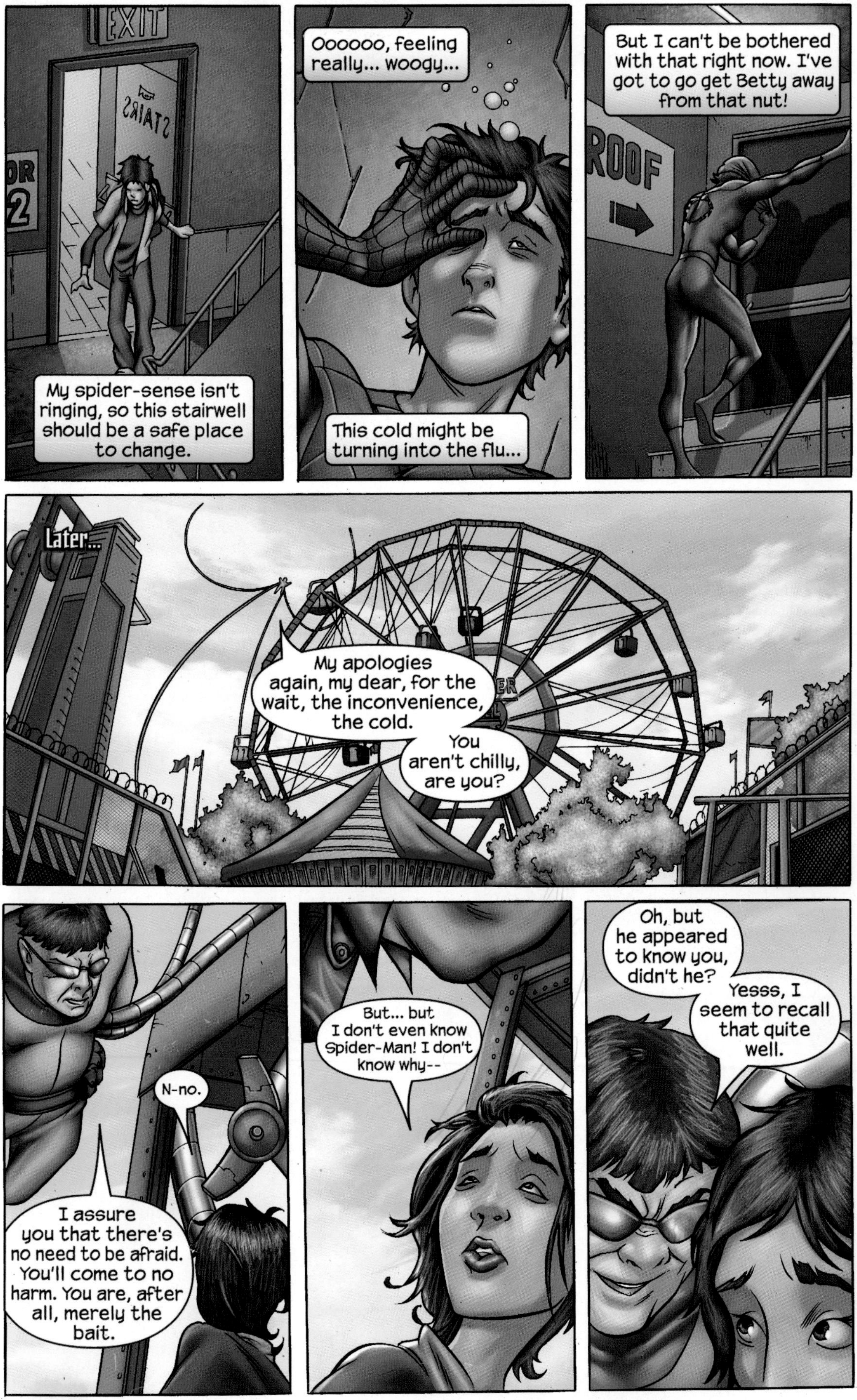
EXIT
STAIRS
My spider-sense isn't ringing, so this stairwell should be a safe place to change.
Oooooo, feeling really... woogy...
This cold might be turning into the flu...
But I can't be bothered with that right now. I've got to go get Betty away from that nut!
ROOF
Later...
My apologies again, my dear, for the wait, the inconvenience, the cold.
You aren't chilly, are you?
N-no.
I assure you that there's no need to be afraid. You'll come to no harm. You are, after all, merely the bait.
But... but I don't even know Spider-Man! I don't know why--
Oh, but he appeared to know you, didn't he?
Yesss, I seem to recall that quite well.

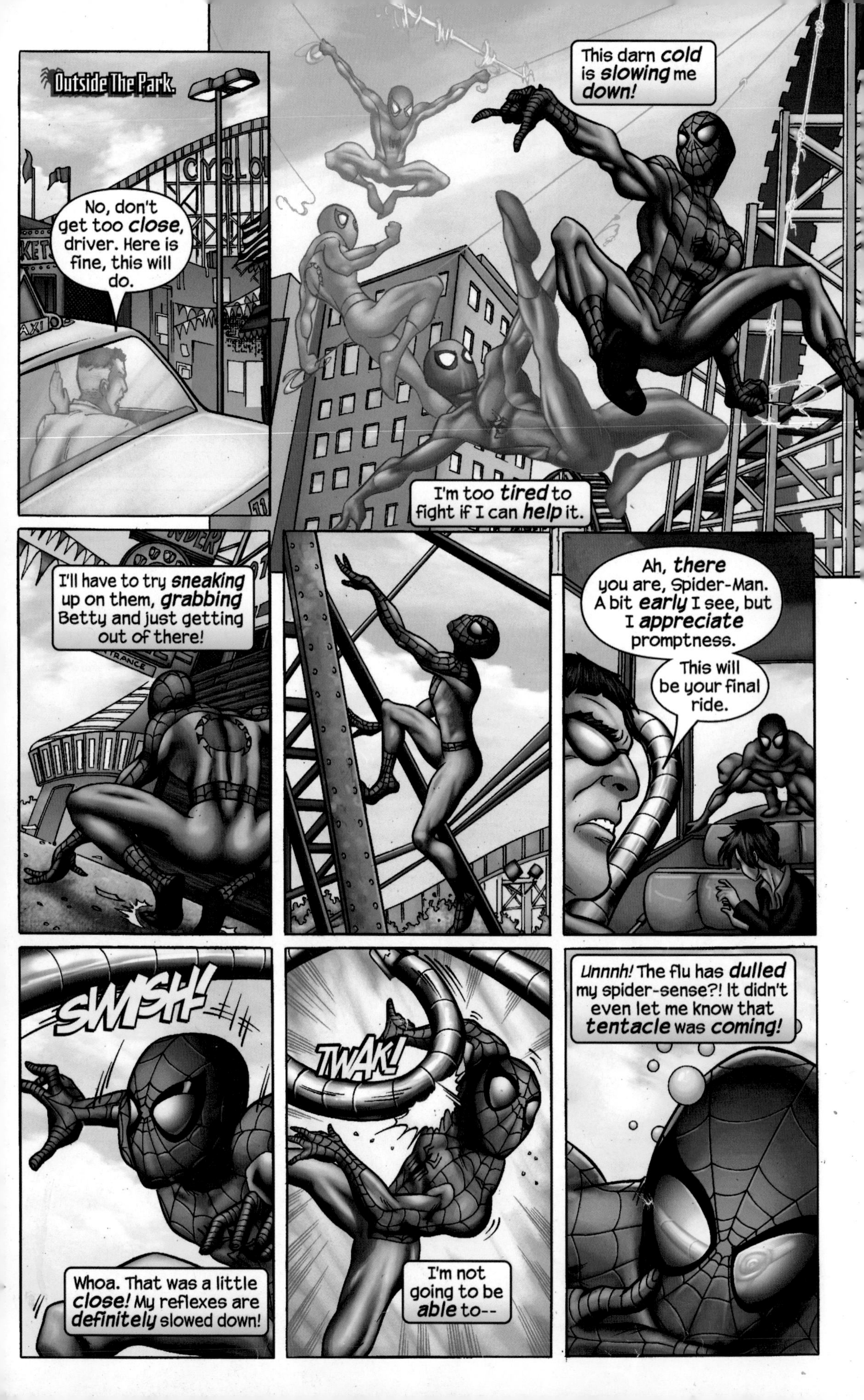
Outside The Park.
CYCLO
No, don't get too close, driver. Here is fine, this will do.
This darn cold is slowing me down!
I'm too tired to fight if I can help it.
I'll have to try sneaking up on them, grabbing Betty and just getting out of there!
Ah, there you are, Spider-Man. A bit early I see, but I appreciate promptness.
This will be your final ride.
SWISH!
Whoa. That was a little close! My reflexes are definitely slowed down!
TWAK!
I'm not going to be able to--
Unnnh! The flu has dulled my spider-sense?! It didn't even let me know that tentacle was coming!

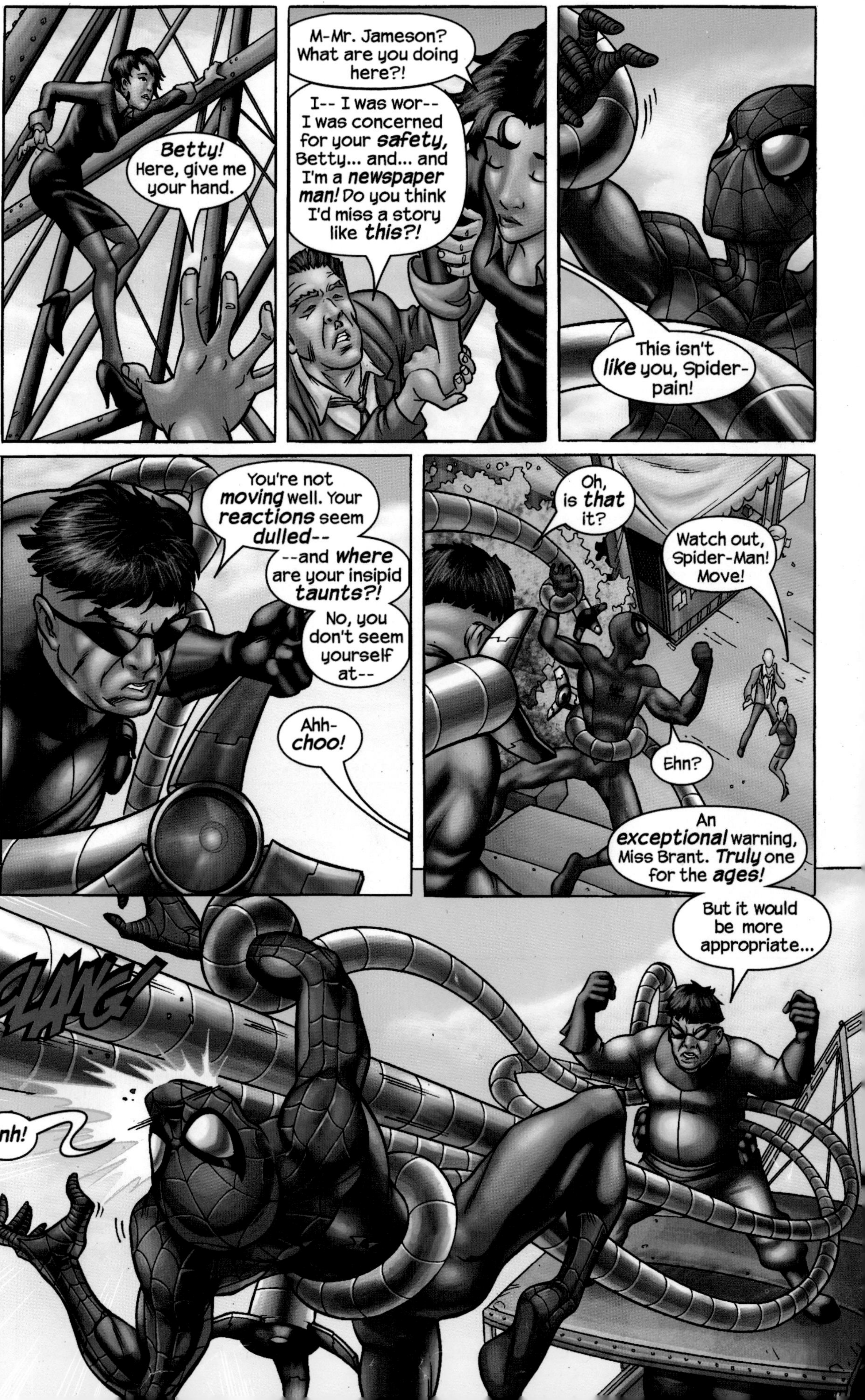
Betty! Here, give me your hand.
M-Mr. Jameson? What are you doing here?!
I-- I was wor-- I was concerned for your safety, Betty... and... and I'm a newspaper man! Do you think I'd miss a story like this?!
This isn't like you, Spider-pain!
You're not moving well. Your reactions seem dulled--
--and where are your insipid taunts?!
No, you don't seem yourself at--
Ahh-choo!
Oh, is that it?
Watch out, Spider-Man! Move!
Ehn?
An exceptional warning, Miss Brant. Truly one for the ages!
But it would be more appropriate...
CLANG!
Unh!

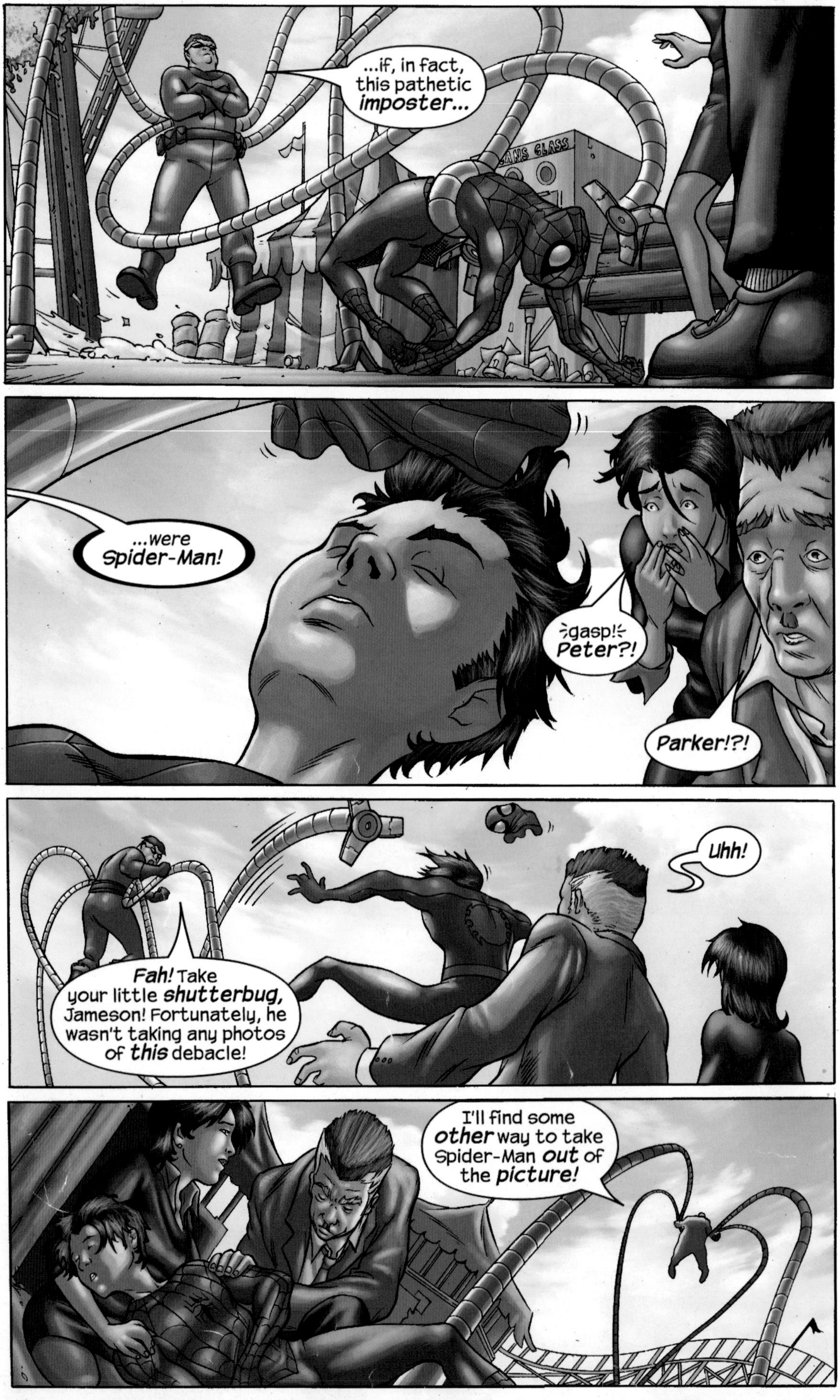
...if, in fact, this pathetic imposter...
...were Spider-Man!
gasp! Peter?!
Parker!?!
Uhh!
Fah! Take your little shutterbug, Jameson! Fortunately, he wasn't taking any photos of this debacle!
I'll find some other way to take Spider-Man out of the picture!

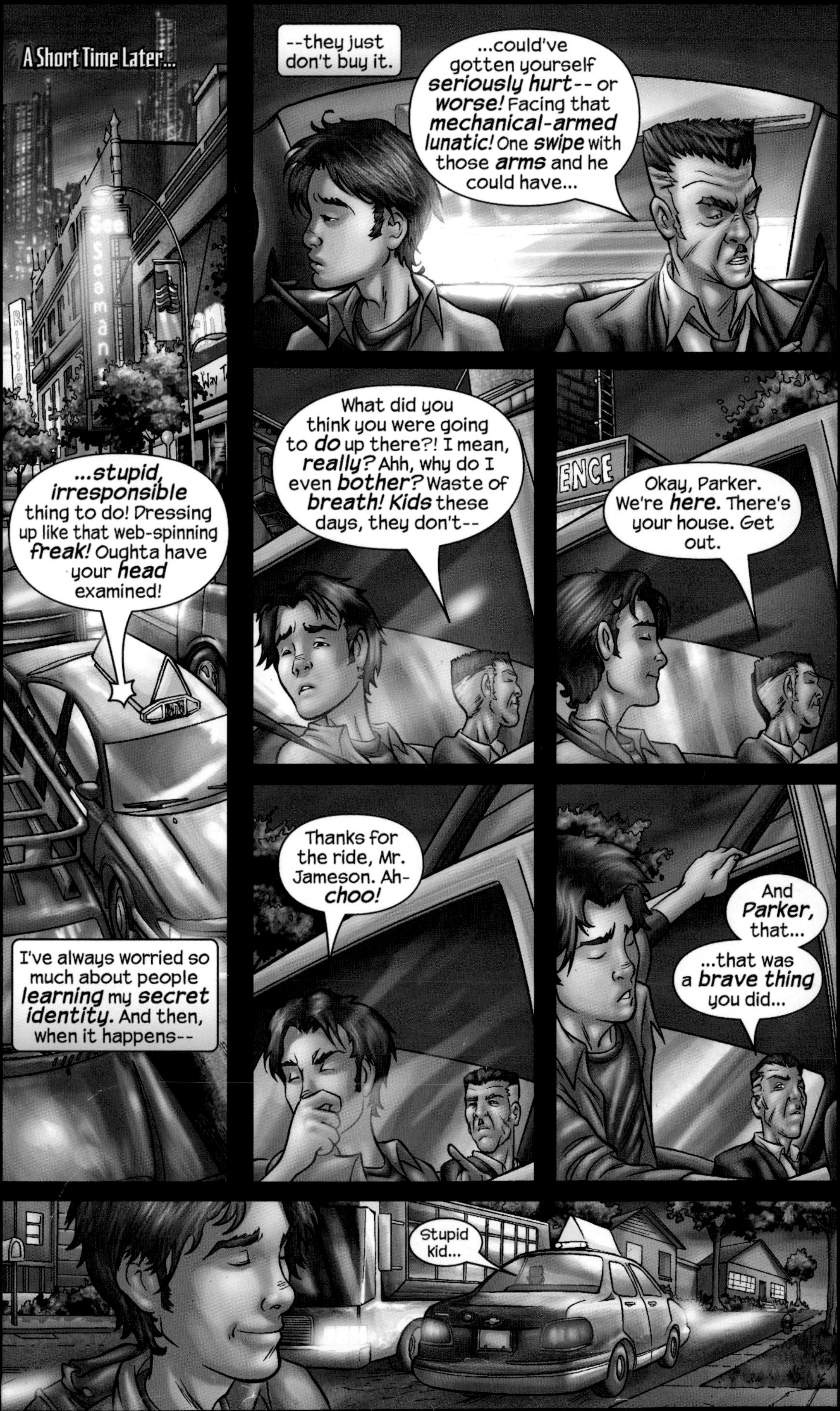
A Short Time Later...
...stupid, irresponsible thing to do! Dressing up like that web-spinning freak! Oughta have your head examined!
I've always worried so much about people learning my secret identity. And then, when it happens--
--they just don't buy it.
...could've gotten yourself seriously hurt-- or worse! Facing that mechanical-armed lunatic! One swipe with those arms and he could have...
What did you think you were going to do up there?! I mean, really? Ahh, why do I even bother? Waste of breath! Kids these days, they don't--
Okay, Parker. We're here. There's your house. Get out.
Thanks for the ride, Mr. Jameson. Ah-choo!
And Parker, that...
...that was a brave thing you did...
Stupid kid...

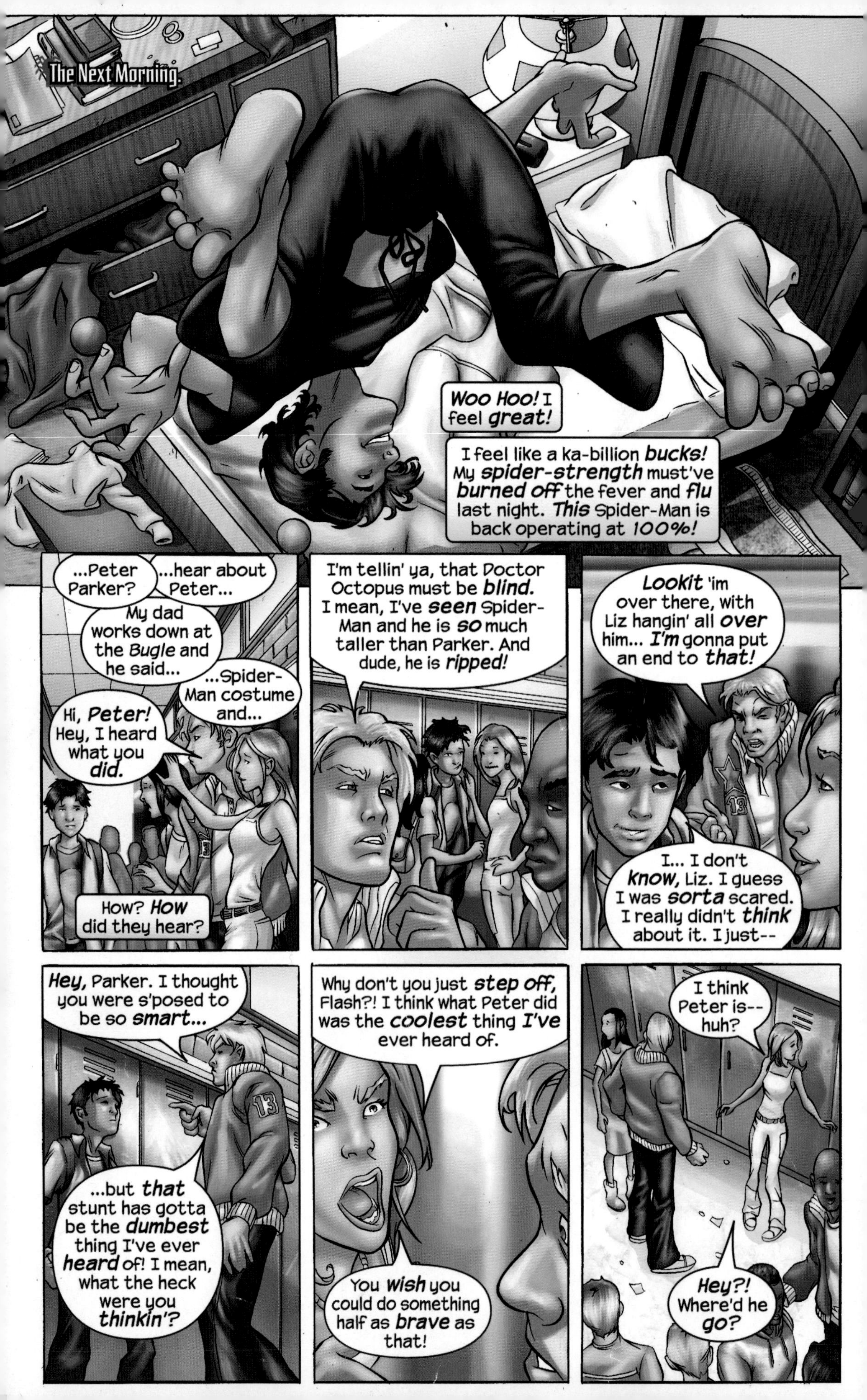

The Next Morning.
Woo Hoo! I feel great!
I feel like a ka-billion bucks! My spider-strength must've burned off the fever and flu last night. This Spider-Man is back operating at 100%!
...Peter Parker?
...hear about Peter...
My dad works down at the Bugle and he said...
...Spider-Man costume and...
Hi, Peter! Hey, I heard what you did.
How? How did they hear?
I'm tellin' ya, that Doctor Octopus must be blind. I mean, I've seen Spider-Man and he is so much taller than Parker. And dude, he is ripped!
Lookit 'im over there, with Liz hangin' all over him... I'm gonna put an end to that!
I... I don't know, Liz. I guess I was sorta scared. I really didn't think about it. I just--
Hey, Parker. I thought you were s'posed to be so smart...
...but that stunt has gotta be the dumbest thing I've ever heard of! I mean, what the heck were you thinkin'?
Why don't you just step off, Flash?! I think what Peter did was the coolest thing I've ever heard of.
You wish you could do something half as brave as that!
I think Peter is-- huh?
Hey?! Where'd he go?

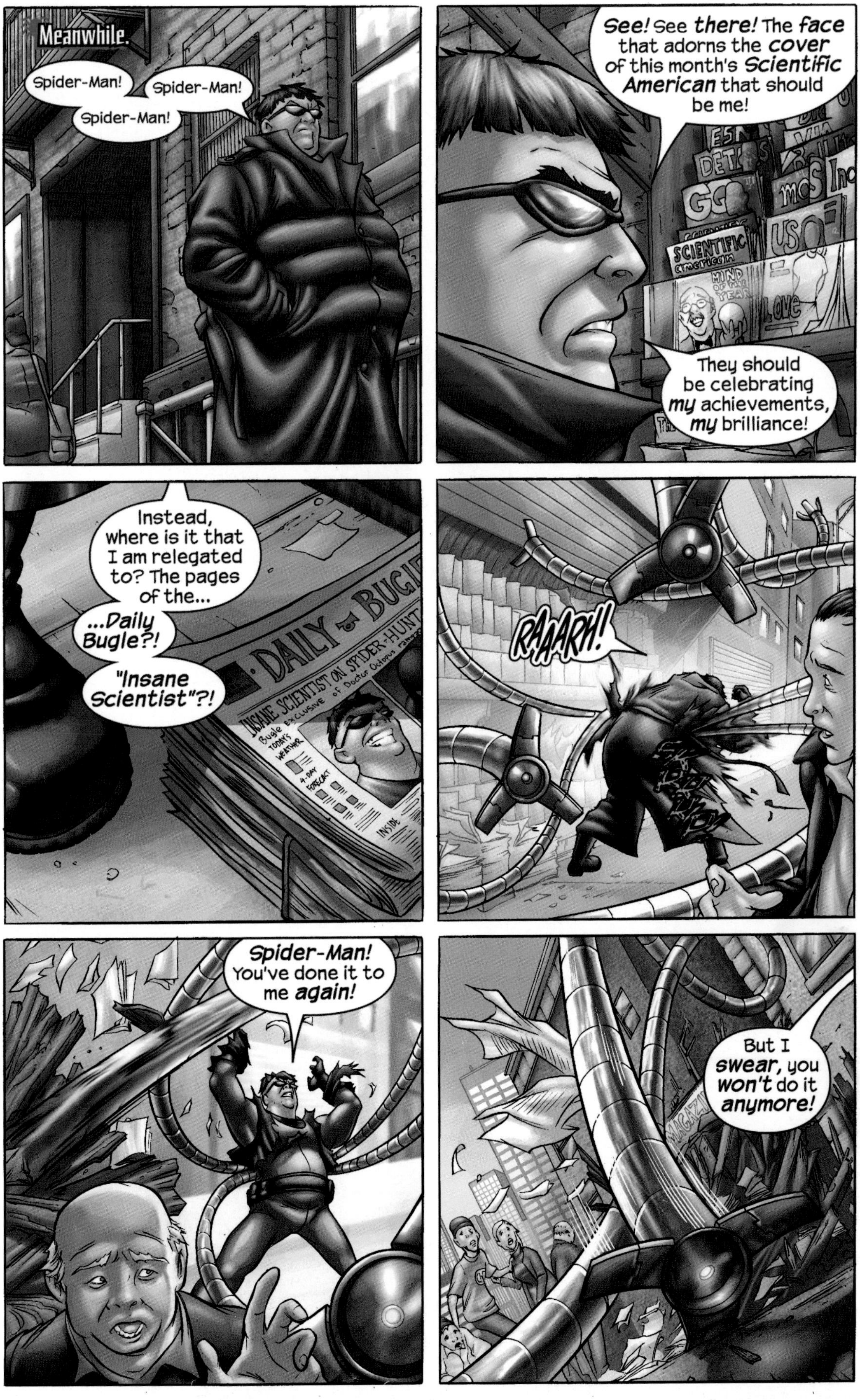
Meanwhile.
Spider-Man!
Spider-Man!
Spider-Man!
See! See there! The face that adorns the cover of this month's Scientific American that should be me!
They should be celebrating my achievements, my brilliance!
Instead, where is it that I am relegated to? The pages of the...
...Daily Bugle?!
"Insane Scientist"?!
RAAARH!
Spider-Man! You've done it to me again!
But I swear, you won't do it anymore!

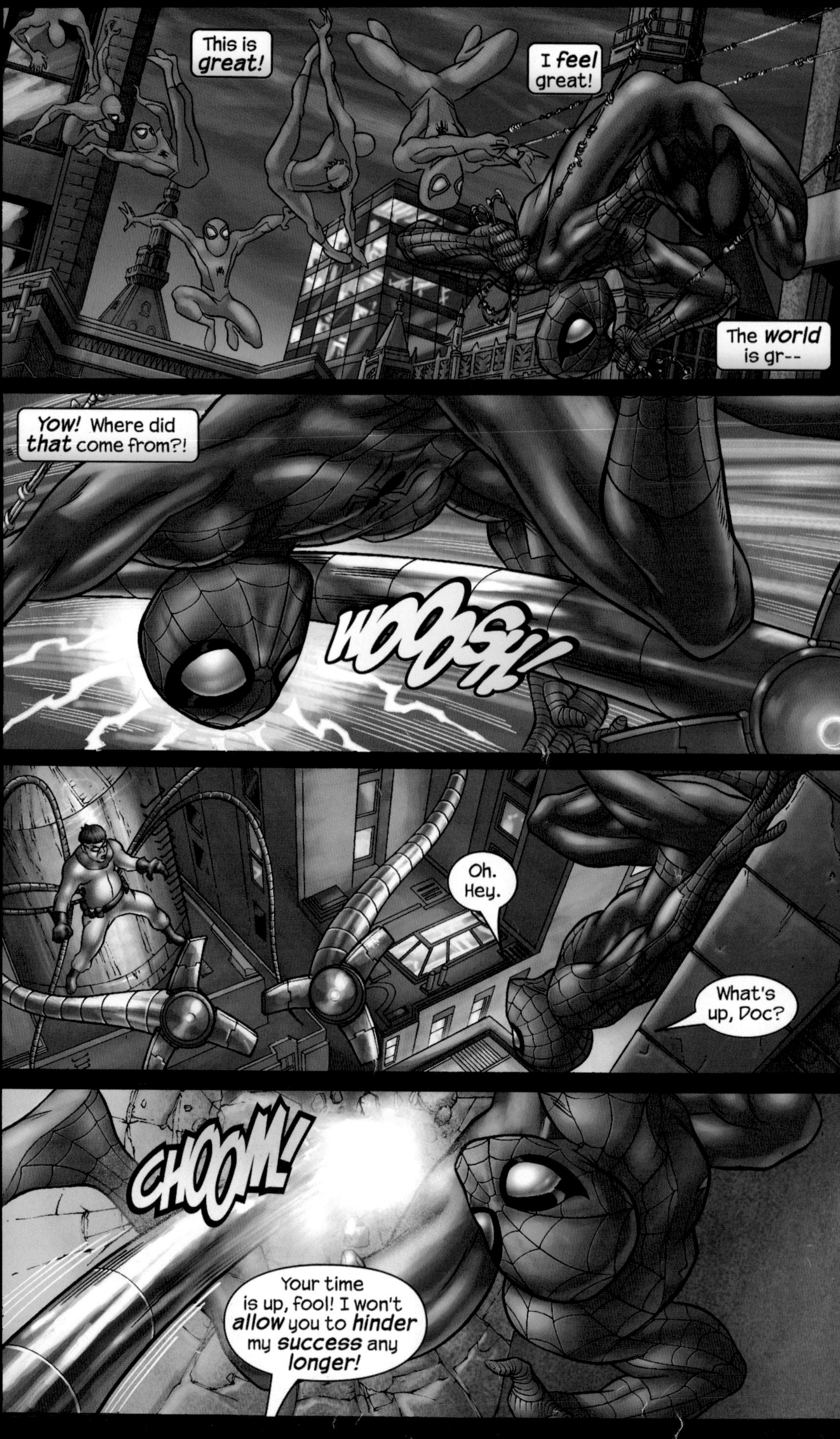

This is great!
I feel great!
The world is gr--
YOW! Where did that come from?!
WOOOSH!
Oh. Hey.
What's up, Doc?
CHOOM!
Your time is up, fool! I won't allow you to hinder my success any longer!

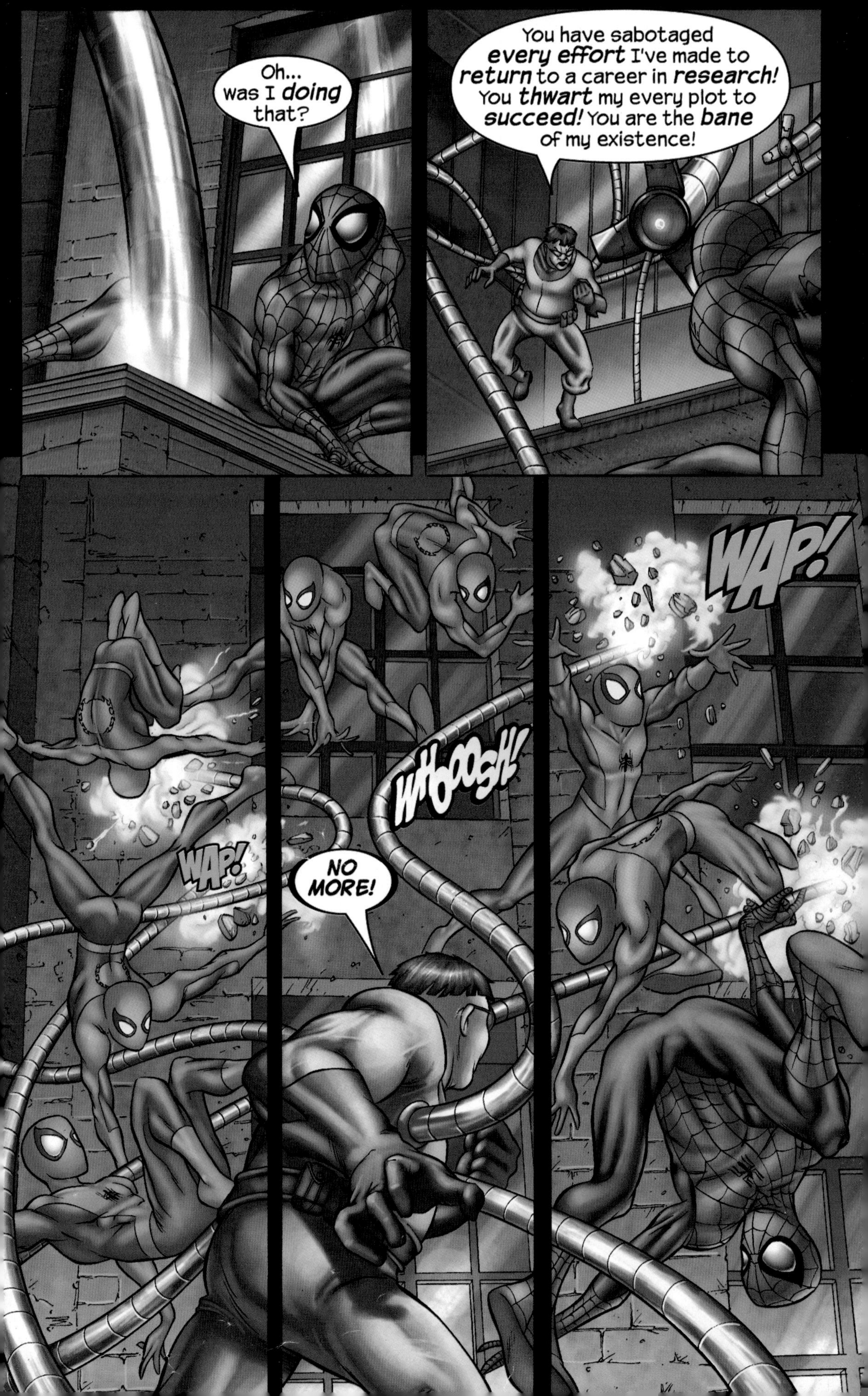
Oh... was I doing that?
You have sabotaged every effort I've made to return to a career in research! You thwart my every plot to succeed! You are the bane of my existence!
WAP!
WHOOOSH!
NO MORE!
WAP!

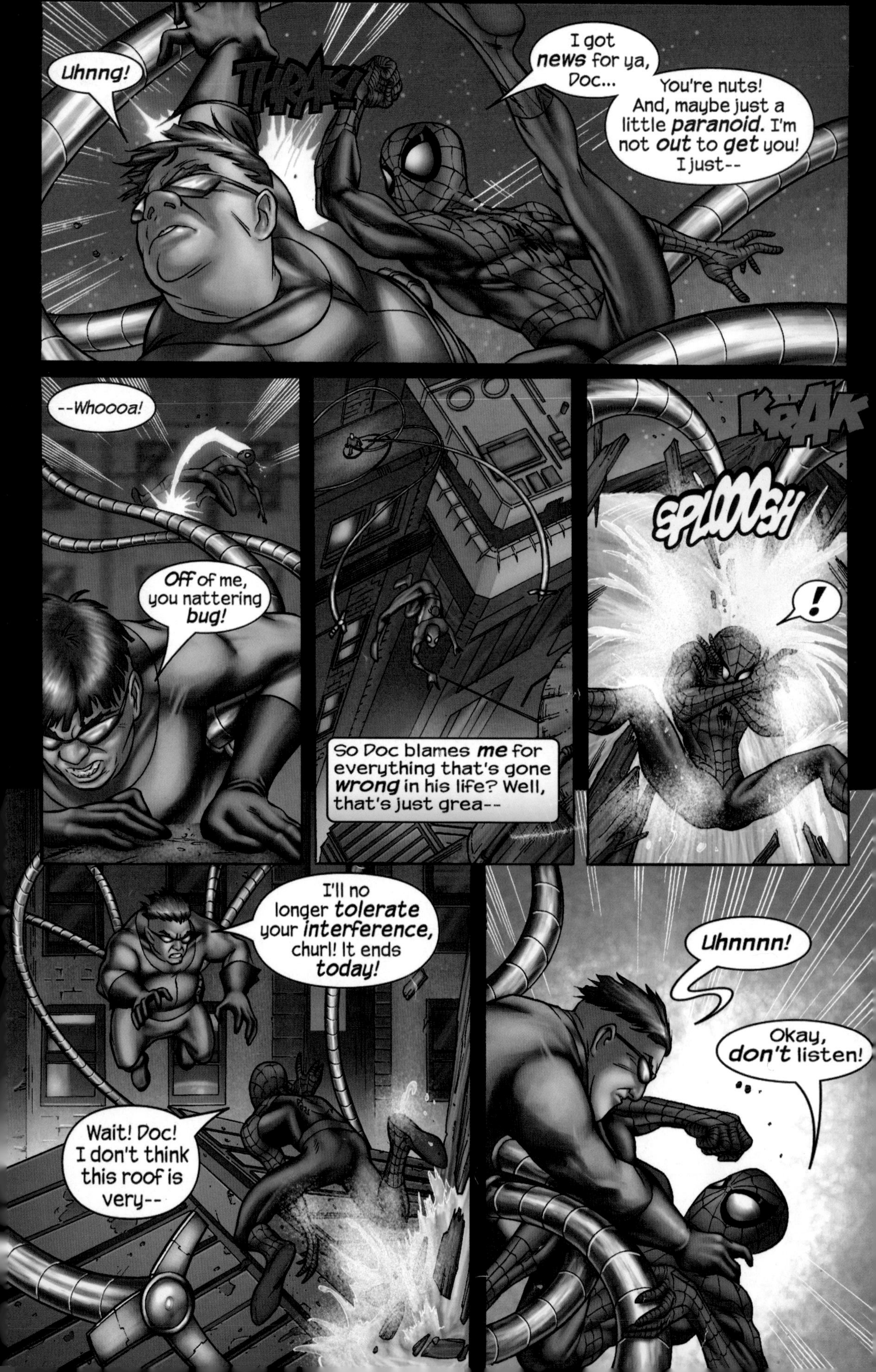

Uhnng!
THRAK!
I got news for ya, Doc...
You're nuts! And, maybe just a little paranoid. I'm not out to get you! I just--
--Whoooa!
Off of me, you nattering bug!
So Doc blames me for everything that's gone wrong in his life? Well, that's just grea--
KRAK
SPLOOOSH
!
I'll no longer tolerate your interference, churl! It ends today!
Wait! Doc! I don't think this roof is very--
Uhnnnn!
Okay, don't listen!

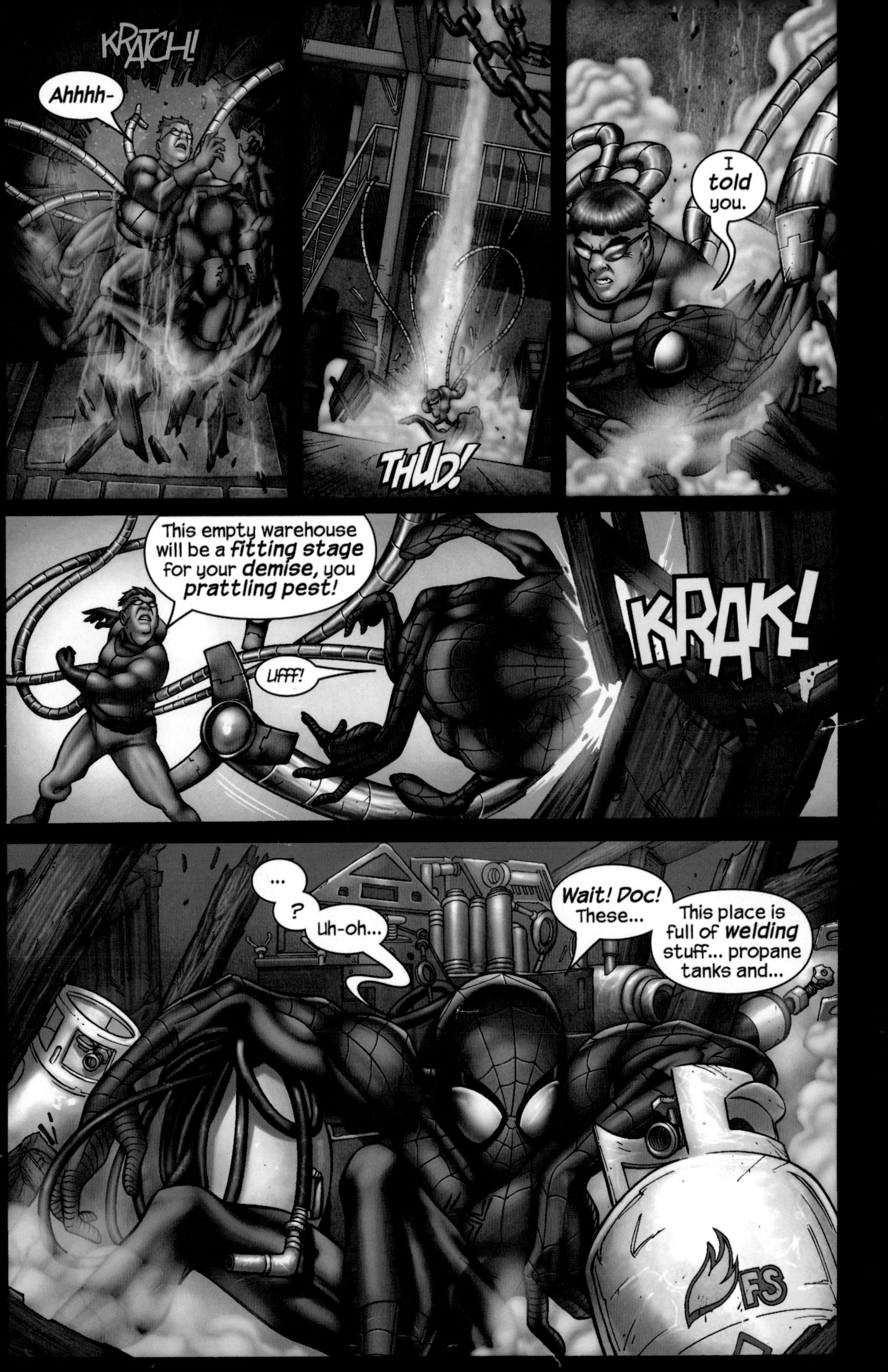
KRATCH!
Ahhhh-
THUD!
I told you.
This empty warehouse will be a fitting stage for your demise, you prattling pest!
UFFF!
KRAK!
...
?
Uh-oh...
Wait! Doc! These...
This place is full of welding stuff... propane tanks and...
FS

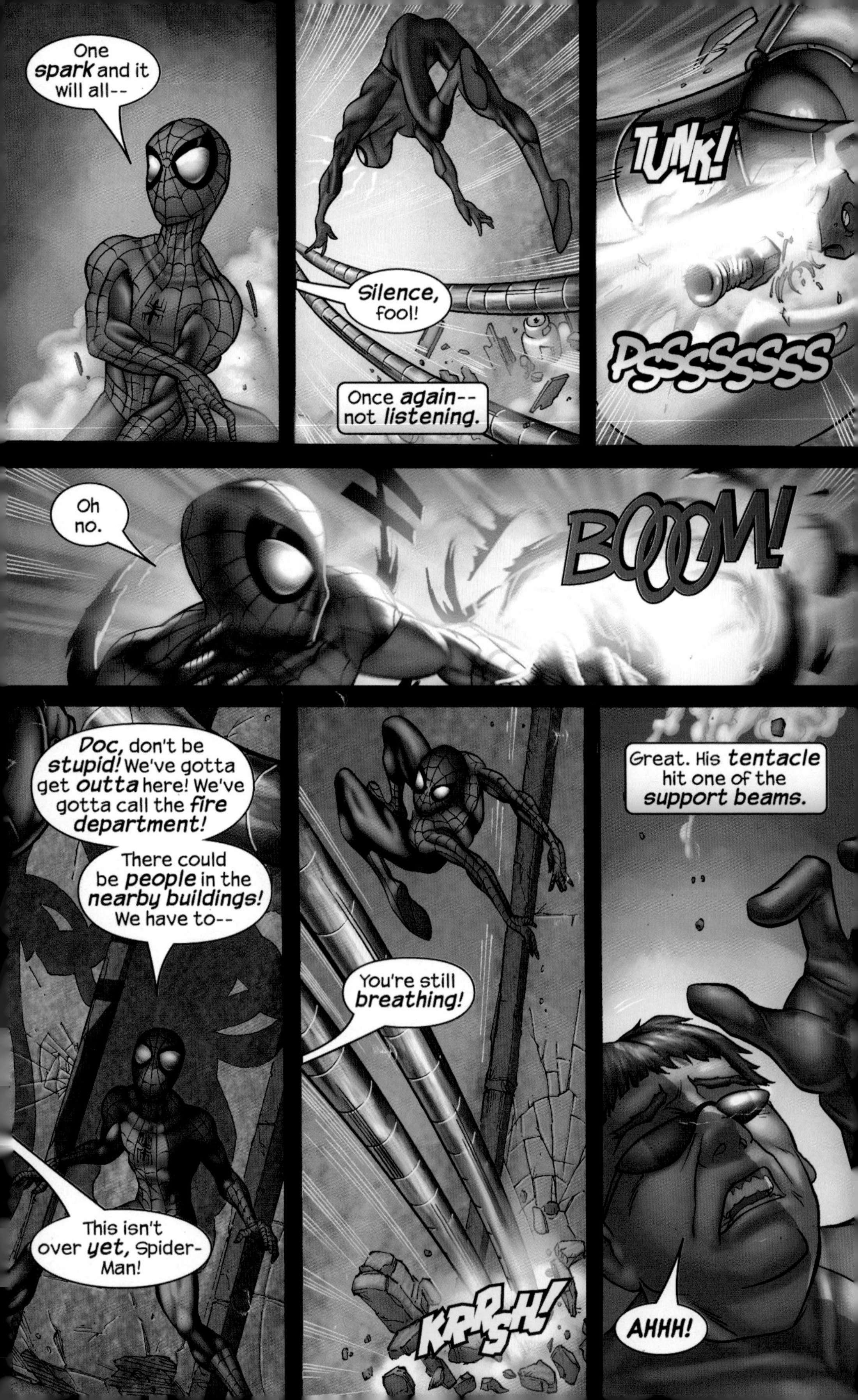
One spark and it will all--
Silence, fool!
Once again--not listening.
TUNK!
PSSSSSSS
Oh no.
BOOOM!
Doc, don't be stupid! We've gotta get outta here! We've gotta call the fire department!
There could be people in the nearby buildings! We have to--
This isn't over yet, Spider-Man!
You're still breathing!
KRRSH!
Great. His tentacle hit one of the support beams.
AHHH!

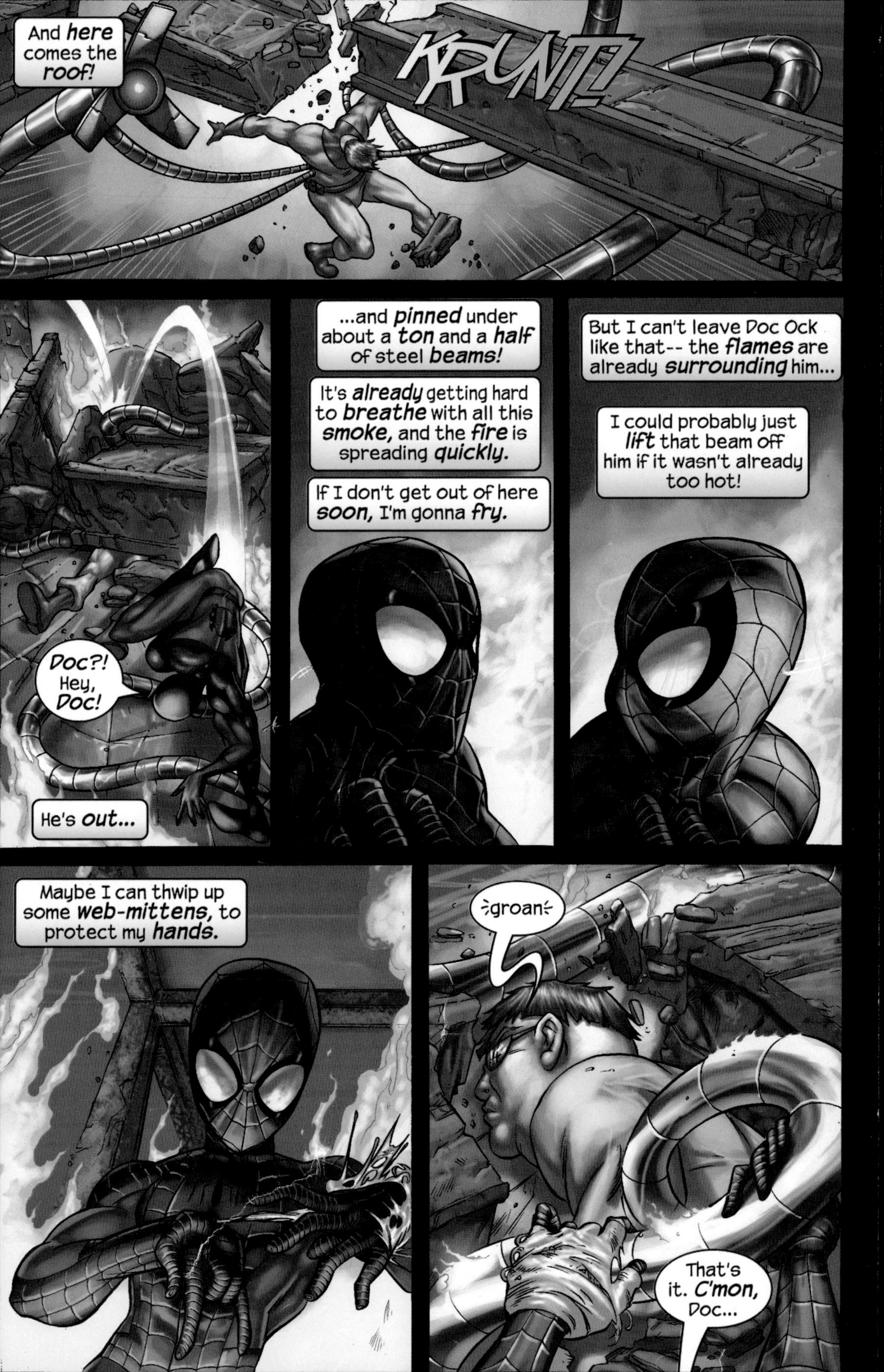

And here comes the roof!
KRUNTT!
...and pinned under about a ton and a half of steel beams!
It's already getting hard to breathe with all this smoke, and the fire is spreading quickly.
If I don't get out of here soon, I'm gonna fry.
Doc?! Hey, Doc!
He's out...
But I can't leave Doc Ock like that-- the flames are already surrounding him...
I could probably just lift that beam off him if it wasn't already too hot!
Maybe I can thwip up some web-mittens, to protect my hands.
groan
That's it. C'mon, Doc...

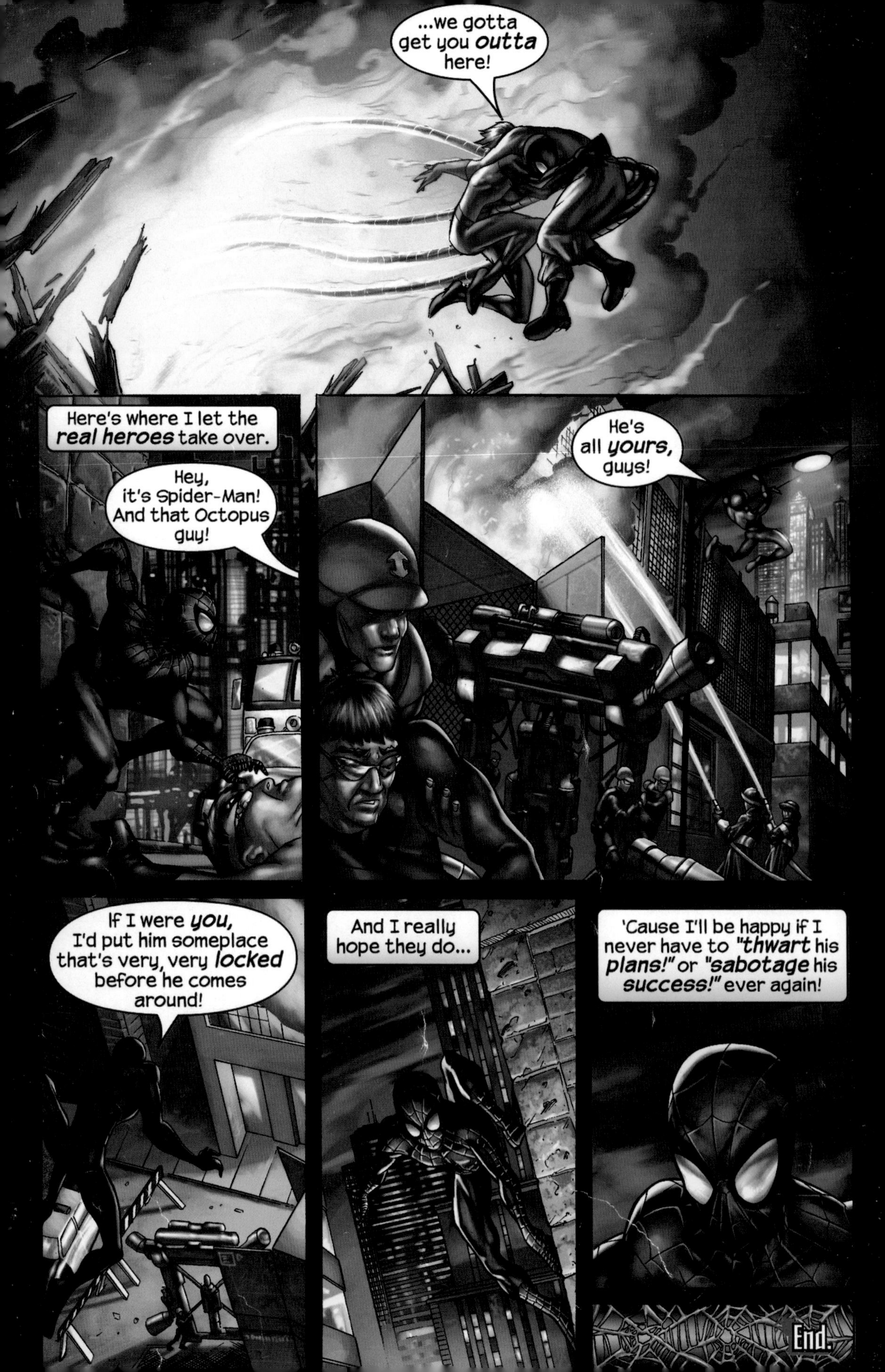

...we gotta get you *outta* here!
Here's where I let the *real heroes* take over.
Hey, it's Spider-Man! And that Octopus guy!
He's all *yours,* guys!
If I were *you,* I'd put him someplace that's very, very *locked* before he comes around!
And I really hope they do...
'Cause I'll be happy if I never have to *"thwart* his *plans!"* or *"sabotage* his *success!"* ever again!
End.